My Teacher's as Wild as a Bison

Dedicated to Charlie and Andy, at the beginning of their journey together

MY TEACHER'S AS WILD AS A BISON

AND OTHER POEMS BASED ON THE GREAT OUTDOORS

Coral Rumble

Illustrated by Nigel Baines

LION
CHILDREN'S

Text copyright © 2005 Coral Rumble
Illustrations copyright © 2005 Nigel Baines
This edition copyright © 2005 Lion Hudson

The moral rights of the author and illustrator
have been asserted

A Lion Children's Book
an imprint of
Lion Hudson plc
Mayfield House, 256 Banbury Road,
Oxford OX2 7DH, England
www.lionhudson.com
ISBN 0 7459 4954 1

First edition 2005
10 9 8 7 6 5 4 3 2 1 0

Acknowledgments
The poems on the following pages were first published thus: page 52 in *The
Poetry Store*, Paul Cookson (ed.), Hodder Wayland, 2005; page 56 in *Christmas
Poems*, Gaby Morgan (ed.), Macmillan, 2003; page 59 in *Frogs in Clogs*, Gaby
Morgan (ed.), Macmillan, 2005; page 70 in *Hey Diddle Riddle*, John Foster (ed.),
OUP, 2003.

A catalogue record for this book is available
from the British Library

Typeset in 12/14 Latin 725 BT
Printed and bound in Great Britain
by Cox & Wyman Ltd, Reading

CONTENTS

A note from the author 9

Raft building 11

Canoe race 12

Water shoot 13

View from a bridge 14

Voice 15

Sighting at Loch Ness 16

Cave music 18

Point of view 19

The rock climber's poem 20

At the rock face 21

Applause 22

One poem about two falls 23

Gull on the school roof 24

Crow 25

Scarecrow 26

Bat in a barn 27

Dancer 28

Wildcat 29

A tale of fur and feathers 30

Dog training 31

Haiku riddle bugs 32

Beetle lout   34

Just a suggestion   35

Maytime twister   36

This poem is quite a let-down   37

Cosmic questions   38

Return from school camp   40

Poem for the Head of Geography   41

Walkabout   44

Stitched up   45

Ache   46

The wall   47

Park game   48

On the deck   49

Exhibition   50

Dying embers   51

Snow flurry   52

Winter spikes   53

School closure   54

Street lights   56

Spring   57

Summer paddling   58

Seasoned cinquains   59

Magic string   60

Polite   61

Divine intervention on an OFSTED day   62

The heavens open   64

An English holiday   66

Daydream   68

Glimpse   69

Make a quick guess   70

Warning   71

Piranha drama   72

The mask   73

Diving for Daniel   74

Wreck   76

Freak   78

Zap   79

Armadillo pillow   80

Excuse   81

My teacher's as wild as a bison   82

The Colorado diet   85

Contaminated   86

Polar problem   87

Pity at a car boot sale   88

Aslan rising   89

Potty   90

That's entertainment   91

Dancing bear   92

Gus   93

Wild about teeth   94

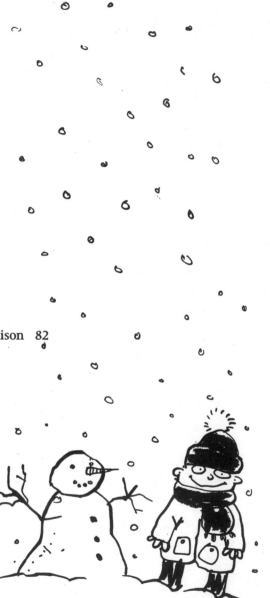

A note from the author

Do you like to laugh? So do I! I like to write poems that make people laugh, too. You can tell from the title that *My Teacher's as Wild as a Bison* contains some funny poems, but you can expect much more than that! Poems may make us laugh, but they can also make us cry, feel scared or good about ourselves. Some poems make us think until our brains ache, or make us feel until our hearts break.

In this collection of poems you'll be taken on a journey around the world to experience the great outdoors. You will climb hills, watch creatures in the woods, and notice the countryside in the city. Be careful – at one stage the weather gets very changeable. You'll go on school camp with friends, and then stand in the playground – all alone. And if you've time for more excitement, you'll dive down into the ocean to visit a shipwreck, and then, a few pages later, stand on an African plain.

Reading these poems will also take you on another journey – one that happens inside you as you laugh, cry, fear, think and feel. ENJOY THE RIDE!

Raft building

words   *so grab some words and rope them on,*   are like a raft   *there are pages and pages to sail upon.*   you build;

once they're   linked and holes   are filled,

they   float you to a   distant place,

where   stories grow and   poems pace;

where verbs   can leap and   nouns can vault,

where   syllables can   somersault;

where   letters can run   wild and free,

then   regroup for a   spelling bee.

Canoe race

The river's skin is a moving canvas, wet with life –
I slow my canoe to inspect the changing images.
First, reeds bend and waver in a ripple;
Then, a water vole dives a black-brown brush stroke
Across the green water's edge, framed with
    meadowsweet;
A yellow-white splash of sunshine colour-washes
    the water shades.
I float on, long streamers of willowmoss trailing
    from my paddle,
And peer down to watch a hundred wriggling
    minnows
Add a new texture to this watercolour.
I am out of stroke with the other canoeists –
The river is their racetrack glide to glory;
They splash their rhythms left, right, left, right,
    left, right.
I am happy to let the lapping water rock me
Into the miniature rhythms of a riverscape.

Water shoot

the village stream chatters;
bubbles gossip together
in an excited jostle,
bursting with news
of high-hill happenings.
the journey has been long:
trickling has been tickling
many thirsty pebbles;
grasses have bowed
in the go of the flow;
hooves have stood firm
in the froth of the rush;
twigs have spun round
in the twirl of the whirl;
leaves have been launched
in the zigzag twist;
and now a fill of water

strokes the hollow of the bridge
on which we stand

to watch the rushing giggle,
and the wriggle of fish
riding the thrill of the slide
and the crash of the splash.

View from a bridge
(a haiku)

The stream is rigid,
It cannot move a ripple –
Wheezing and breathless.

Voice

Under the arches of this bridge,
Where scuttling mice and insects live,
I hear a voice that sounds like mine –
In fact, I've heard it several times.

The voice is mine, yet far away,
It doesn't have that much to say;
In truth, it just repeats itself
And never answers someone else.

So is it my voice, somehow caught
Beneath this span of bricks, so taut?
Perhaps it can escape this hollow –
If I walk out, then will it follow?

Sighting at Loch Ness

I've seen the Ness...
Well, more or less –

The water stirred,
I thought I heard
An eerie moan,
A kind of groan
From down below
The surface flow.

I thought I saw
A flippered paw,
A splashing tail,
Grey, like a whale,
An arch of muscle,
A ripple ruffle.

I strained my eyes
As she swam by,
A shadow passed
On surface glass,
Then went from sight
In fading light.

I've seen the Ness...
Well, more or less.

Cave music

In the echo of the cave,
In the belly of the hill,
I can hear the planet's pulse
As I stand so very still.
I can hear the drip of life,
I can feel the chill of dark,
I can touch the silk of rocks
Where a stream has made its mark.
I can see the glistening arches
In the cavern up ahead,
I can feel the bounce of drips
On the helmet on my head.
I can hear earth's ageless music
As it echoes round the space,
Singing songs of a beginning
When God threw it into place.

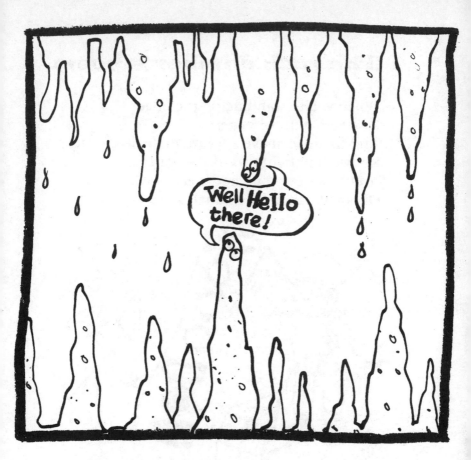

Point of view

(a couplet)

A stalactite grows down in height;
It can't look up, but a stalagmite.

The rock climber's poem

When you're standing on the edge
Of a very narrow ledge,
And the rope above appears to be quite slack,
Respect the tightness of the squeeze
And be sure you do not sneeze,
Or you'll dangle at an angle on your back!

At the rock face

Got me up here!
The courage that
My friends all cheer
My teacher claps,
I didn't drop.
I can't believe
Up to the top,
I slowly climb
Without a fight.
I won't give up
Grip them tight,
I stretch to handholds,
I'm full of dread.
The pressure builds,
Inside my head,
I hear my heart
With too much haste.
No need to climb
Around my waist,
The rope is tied
The world is black.
The others watch,
No going back,
➤ It's my turn next,

Applause

From this old cairn* we can look down
On the track we've been trekking,
On the route we've been stepping,
Through clumps of grass prickles
And under the broken limbs of trees left trailing.
Our leg muscles pulse a fast disco beat.
We sweat out drops of salty determination.
Rucksacks open to spill bottles and boxes.

We retell our journey, unpack the moments.
Talk about the deserted shepherd's hut,
The balance of old stone walls,
The shimmer of distant tarns**,
Until a breeze sweeps our words away.

In the hush of the air, we watch
As pine trees point up to the heavens
And clap their hands.

* A cairn is a pyramid of rough stones to mark a path or another important thing.
** A tarn is a small mountain lake.

One poem about two falls

The funambulist*

though once on top

is in a twist

he now is not.
Instead he hangs
below the rope,
his straining toes
his only hope.
His balance lost
his ego tattered,
his arms hung limp,
his vanity battered.
This latest feat
was a feat too far,
with an upturned view
of Niagara.

* A funambulist is a tightrope-walker.

Gull on the school roof

Gull on the school roof –
Chameleon against the grey, clouded sky,
Sitting with long wings folded,
With head jerking, square tail twitching –
Have you come to remind us of summer?
Of the promise of warm paddling days?
Do you want us to remember, on this blustery day,
The sound of raking shingle,
The plop of thrown pebbles sinking
And your own awk-awk-awk of wave skimming?
Gull on the school roof,
When you return to your salt-air gliding,
And before you fly back to your rough cliff-crag nest,
Stand on a breaker and tell the frothing waves
That, at school, I am dreaming of days by the sea.

Crow

You will have noticed me
Swooping down, hoarsely calling –
A black, oiled sheen of bird.
I dodge telephone wires, skim chimney corners,
Perch on roof top angles and circle over playgrounds.

My business is theft – eggs, fledglings.
I am without conscience,
My mind is as sharp as hooked claws.
I believe in a pecking order,
Survival of the quickest.
Nothing wrong with being an opportunist,
A scavenger, raider, cruel invader.
My reputation hangs on a cloak of terror.

Scarecrow

Scarecrow stands stiffly:
Stiff straw hair,
Stiff stick back,
Stiff stretched arms.
No amount of stuffing
Can disguise his rigid pose;
No costume can bring life,
Not even a baggy jacket,
Hung haphazardly.
Scarecrow stares straight ahead,
He has no choice.
His eyes don't see, just as
His heart doesn't beat.
But at dusk, when house lights warm the hills,
His stitched mouth droops at the edges,
And his stare softens to a glaze.

I'm glad his ears can't hear
The lonely whispering of the wind
Or the mocking squawk of circling birds.

Bat in a barn

Bat in a barn means no harm –
But a creaking door will cause alarm,
And if his rubbery membranes spread,
A staring child will fill with dread,
And, very soon, will think he sees
An evil glint wink from the eaves,
And then he'll run, with tales to tell
Of cruel, hooked thumbs and toes, and swell
His story to a nightmare size –
But those who know, those who are wise,
Will see that, on the average farm,
Bat in a barn means no harm.

Dancer

In a hollow tree the otter sits –
Wire whiskers twitching,
Head held still in ballerina pose,
Listening for the rustle of a hunter's walk,
For the splash of a stone from passing boys,
For an alien call from hungry lips.
His thick, brown fur trembles,
His body shudders from flattened head
To tapered tail.
Webbed feet root to the spot.
But when the dusk has settled,
And night-time calls meet his own
Thin, high-pitched whistle,
River reeds part
And the dancer slides
Into underwater steps
And a pirouette of bubbles.

Wildcat

Over the rocky heights
Glides the caterwaul of a wildcat.
Her scream cuts through pine needles,
Spiking the forest floor with shafts of menace.
The haunting sound invades the mind,
Turns blood cold, catches the breath
Of night-time ramblers.
Witch of the wild screeches her call,
Hisses through icicle teeth
A cold knife-edge of spite.
Walk quickly and control imagination
With commonsense thoughts of
Her small, leggy build and blunt-ended tail.
Don't look up to the rockface
In case you see a halted, grey shadow
Tinged with the glimmer of moon-glow,
And frosted eyes fixed
On your stumbling ascent.

A tale of fur and feathers

The minky pooka* scales the wall,
Hunches low and holds his call,
Then silently he slinks his way
Towards his witless, bobbing prey.

The minky pooka's eyes fix straight
Towards the target on the gate,
Then, like a laser, his gaze cuts round
To trace her hopping on the ground.

The minky pooka licks his lips,
His whiskers wobble, his nostrils twitch;
His tail springs up, his claws flick wide –
The victim has no place to hide!

The minky pooka fluffs his fur,
Shuts his eyes and starts to purr.
He has no shame, shows no regret,
For his attack, for what he ate.

So, if you fly and hop around,
Be cautious when you hear *no* sound,
For in the shadows around your hopping
A minky pooka might be watching.

* What is a minky pooka? Perhaps you can invent new names for other creatures.

Dog training

My dog digs in the garden,
It makes my mum so cross;
He buries things, so gets the blame
For any recent loss.

But I'm quite pleased he digs so deep –
One hole and then another,
It gives me hope that one day soon
He'll bury Tom, my brother!

Haiku riddle bugs

1. Menace to greenfly,
   A small, round, red domino,
   Flying away home.

2. Silently he climbs
   2, 4, 6, 8 legs, clinging –
   Soon the scream will come!

3. Full of leaves, at rest.
   Camping in a silken tent,
   Waiting for rebirth.

4. Shiny, black armour.
   Has a taste for leftovers!
   Humming through the air.

5. Wriggling and wiggling:
   A problem in the kitchen,
   A fisherman's friend.

(Answers: 1. Ladybird, 2. Spider, 3. Caterpillar, 4. Dung beetle, 5. Maggot.)

Beetle lout

Weevil snout
Sticking out
Elephantine
Beetle lout.

There's no yield
In any field
That can produce
A weevil shield.

Just a suggestion

If you hide a
Garden spider
Deep inside your
Sister's drawer,

He might zap her,
Quickly wrap her,
And then trap her
In his jaws!

Maytime twister

(tongue twister)

How high may a mayfly fly?
'Cause a mayfly may fly high.
Suppose a mayfly might
Fly a mayfly height –
For a mayfly that height's high!

This poem is quite a let-down

hot-air balloon
bulging above the hilltops,
coated with the shine of cloud juice.
you dress the sky with a splash of adventure;
your sashes of colour swell the day into joy;
celebrate the height of soundless flight.
you lift and drift, and drift and lift,
until what was elated
and so highly rated
sits sadly negated –
deflated.

Cosmic questions

Under the night sky, in the still, cool night,
I count the pinprick spots of light,
And wonder at the awesome sight,
And what could be beyond

beyond

In my classroom, in the midday sun,
I count the planets one by one,
And wonder how long time has spun
And what could be beyond

beyond

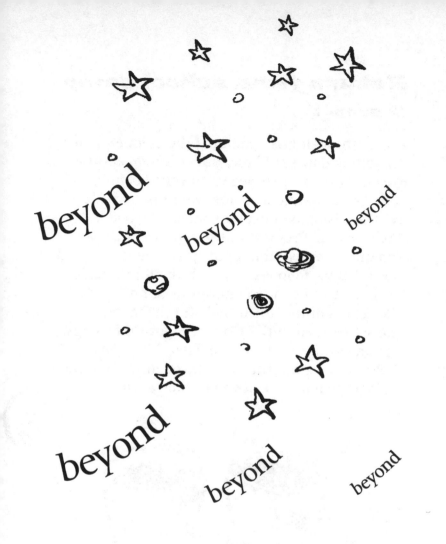

Return from school camp
(a sonnet)

I stare through glass and hear the engine's roar
As, jolting down the lane, our coach makes tracks.
We shudder to a road we've travelled before;
A week has passed and now we must go back.
We leave behind our cabins made of wood,
The warming fires we lit, the rafts we made,
The mud that fell from boots just where we stood,
The maps we followed through the forest glade.
We take with us the memories of camp,
The echoes of the lunch hall and the night,
The smiles seen in the glow of night-time lamps,
The knowledge that we managed things just right.
　　But now I stare and stare through windowpane,
　　Eager to touch the love of home again.

Poem for the Head of Geography

(a ballad)

Head of Geography, Mr Jim Leech,
Took us on a field trip to study a beach.
We stared into rock pools and dug in the sand,
We sketched a few rocks, it all went as planned.

Until, from the waves, to our great surprise,
A green slimy monster, with goggly eyes,
Climbed over the seaweed and onto the shingle;
Our mouths gaped and gasped, our necks cooled and
    tingled.

But Head of Geography, Mr Jim Leech,
Was quite unaware of the 'thing' on the beach;
He squinted at shells and prodded through weed...
We wondered at what time such monsters might
    feed!

The monster approached, we all stepped back,
He hunched up his shoulders and rounded his back.
We thought he would pounce, we thought he would
    dive,
We thought we'd be lucky to be found alive!

But Head of Geography, Mr Jim Leech,
Continued to study, continued to teach.
He talked about landforms with unbridled passion,
While we stood quite rooted, our faces now ashen.

The green slimy monster lumbered around,
Approached Mr Leech, who had only just found
A fossil of interest, and perfectly set,
'Come class, see this, we've not finished yet.'

Head of Geography, Mr Jim Leech,
Was still unaware of the thing on the beach;
Was quite unaware that, leaning over his shoulder,
Was a green slimy monster as large as a boulder.

We discussed if the monster would eat us with salad
(Which could turn this into a healthier ballad),
When, without a growl or flash of his teeth,
He dashed to the waves and plunged down beneath.

Then Head of Geography, Mr Jim Leech,
Looked up from his rock pool and started a speech,
'I'm so disappointed,' and then he got fervent,
'You must pay attention and be more observant!'

Walkabout

Who pushed the poppy through the crack
In the pavement down our street?
Who dangled ivy from the bike shed
Where the kids from round here meet?
Who squeezed the toadstool through the concrete
At the edge of the car park sprawl?
Who spread the moss on the brick-face
Of the crumbling garage wall?
Who nudged the daisy through the tarmac
To make us stop and stare?
Perhaps it was God going walkabout
With a seed-bag of wonder to spare.

Stitched up

I'm a cross cross-country runner,
My knees are caked in mud;
Some run with glee, but oh, not me,
It's just not in my blood.

I'm a slow cross-country runner
Without a race-plan thought;
Five minutes in, my breath is thin,
I start to cough and snort.

I'm a soaked cross-country runner,
My shirt's stuck to my tum,
My shorts are wet and clingy
And sticking to my bum.

I'm a cold cross-country runner,
I shiver in each ditch;
As other runners leap well clear,
I nurse a stabbing stitch.

I'm the last cross-country runner
With sides about to split,
So in defeat I join the heap
Of the hopelessly unfit!

Ache

When teams are picked for playground games,
I never seem to hear my name.

I stand and watch the choices made
And, one by one, my hopes all fade.

I look around, and force a smile,
Lean on the chain-link fence awhile.

I say, as they all race away,
I didn't really want to play.

But, deep inside the pit of me,
I ache an ache no one can see.

The wall

There was a long line of them –
The boys from Brook Street,
No gaps, just solid wall –
And I had to pass,
It was late,
Night would fall.

There was a long line of them
With fists and narrow eyes,
No smiles, just solid hate –
And I had to pass,
If I hid
They would wait.

Park game

My brother races up the wing –
He scores, they roar
And shout and sing –
But they won't let me play.

Ben begins a new attack,
With pace to chase
Defenders back –
But they won't let me play.

I watch them play with heart and soul;
They pass with class
Another goal! –
But they won't let me play.

Later on, my dad comes out;
They win, he grins,
I stare and pout –
'Cause they didn't let me play.

On the deck

(a kennings poem)

Air slider
Pipe glider
Edge skimmer
Truck spinner
Kick flipper
Bench clipper
Space twister
Ground resister
Ramp climber
Pace timer
Stair skier
Limb freer
Tail grabber
Tech-term babbler
Deck lifter
Speed shifter
Vert trickster
Move mixer
Smooth cruiser
Skill enthuser
Stunt glider
Crowd divider.

Exhibition

This cobwebbed fence is saved from being ordinary,
On a frosty morning of icy waking.
Instead, this garden divider, barrier provider,
Is an art gallery, hung with silver-spun originals.
Brush strokes are suspended in the air, canvasless.
Thin lines shiver into diamond etchings.
The grey air fractures with dog barks and milk bottle
  clinks,
With the skedaddle of cats in an alleyway
And the persistent turning of a car engine.
A new day is stirring and soon
A schoolboy will pass, stop, look and marvel
At the patterns of spiders.

Dying embers

Autumn spins a golden web over trees, fields, valleys.
She breathes out a warm rustling and leaves drop.
She winks an orange eye, spreads her amber fingers
   wide.
She scatters the taste of cinnamon and coffee,
The shades of walnut and almond, caramel and
   toffee.
She flies from north to south, east to west,
Riding on a wild wind that bucks and rears like
   a stallion,
Until her great mahogany shadow soaks the land.
Things crumble, things sleep, things die,
And we are reminded that, under heaven,
There is a time and season for everything.

Snow flurry

Snowflakes rushing,
Children hushing,
Corners fluffing –
Cotton-wooled.
People walking,
People stalking,
Slipping, sliding,
Being fooled.
Falling over,
Falling under,
Falling, falling
Down and down;
Making footprints,
Making handprints,
In the white tints
Of the town.

Winter spikes

When Winter comes he bares his teeth,
Watch out he doesn't bite you.
He'll open wide his mouth and SNAP –
On icicles he'll spike you!

School closure

The sky is falling,
The grass is white,
My garden looks
An awesome sight –
And there's no school today!

The trees have caught
The snowflake flurry,
No one's walking
In a hurry –
And there's no school today!

The pond is frozen,
The path is ice,
But today our town
Looks twice as nice –
And there's no school today!

Bushes are bending,
Iced like cakes,
What a difference
Snowflakes make! –
And there's no school today!

A robin hops
And makes a track –
Ten bobs forward,
Ten bobs back –
And there's no school today!

My gloves are wet,
My fingers burn,
Today a snowman
Will help me learn –
'CAUSE THERE'S NO SCHOOL TODAY… HOORAY!

Street lights

The town leapt a little, tonight,
As the Christmas lights came on.
Everyday streets became more important
And even the darkest pathways glistened.
Stars and snowflakes,
Angels and reindeer,
Flashed and flickered a holy-white whisper,
Making our town,
Our ordinary, brick and tarmac town,
Sparkle like a frosted castle
In a far-off, frozen land.

Spring

(a kennings poem)

Sun waker
Music maker
Bud popper
Bird hopper
Crocus grower
Shoot shower
Daffodil dabbler
Brook babbler
Breeze puffer
Petal fluffer
Duckweed floater
Blossom bloater
Cuckoo spotter
Flowerbed plotter
Leaf sprouter
Out and abouter
Stream rusher
Waterfall gusher
Lamb lifter
Cloud drifter
Squirrel tumbler
Bee bumbler
Butterfly singer
New life bringer.

Summer paddling

Twee-wee-wee is the sandpiper's song,
With his slender beak and his legs so long.
His reflection shivers on the water's skin
As he wades on legs that are knobble-kneed
    thin.

He bobs his head; he bobs his tail,
Paddling and probing a mud-covered snail.
In mountain loch he struts and pokes,
Muddying water with weed-bed smoke.

Twee-wee-wee is the sandpiper's song,
Intruder wary, all summer long.
Green-brown blending among the reeds,
Little stilt-walker of summer's first breeze.

Seasoned cinquains

Autumn
Tinge of henna
Crackling fires and leaves
Deep rooting tick of biding time
Digging.

Winter
Stiff morning air
Cracked ice on sleeping seeds
Frosty breath shiver-shudders words
Waiting.

Spring air
Fairy-wing breeze
Lifting blossom petals
Weightless whispering of summer
Stirring.

Summer
Claiming a crown
Exploding wild colours
In a frenzy of patterning
Clapping.

Magic string

I saw a kite above a field,
It climbed and flapped and fell.
A little boy held in his hand
Some string, which I could tell
Would make the kite do special tricks,
And twist and turn and loop the loop;
Jump autumn clouds and ride the wind,
And dive into an eagle swoop,
Until the wind moved on from there
And left the sky ice-cold and bare.

To God
Here
There
Everywhere
Europe, Earth
The Universe
~~#~~ Always

Polite

Dear God, I thought I'd write to you
A thank you note for all you do.
I've noticed that each plant and tree
Has been crafted individually.
And every person that I meet
Is special, different, quite unique!
The sun was such a good idea,
Not far away, yet not too near.
It must have taken days of planning,
Double-checking, blueprint scanning,
Until you got the whole world right,
Divided up the day and night.
And how do you keep the whole thing
  working?
You never sleep, you're never shirking!
So I thought I really ought to write.
(I've been brought up to be polite!)

Divine intervention on an OFSTED day

'It's blowing a gale out there,' she said,
'It's blowing a gale today;
The roof of the office has flipped and crashed –
The inspector is floating away!'

'The inspector is floating away!' she said,
'Over trees and roof tops and cars;
He's moving at quite a speed now,
Suppose he could go very far.'

'Suppose he could go very far,' she said,
'Arms and legs spread in the air,
Hovering over your parents' heads
While they look up and stare!'

'While they look up and stare,' she said,
'I expect he'll shout and wave.
Perhaps they'll throw a line to him,
Perhaps he will be saved.'

'Perhaps he will be saved,' she said,
'But for now, Class 6, please turn
To page number 9 of your exercise book,
We all have a lesson to learn.'

'We all have a lesson to learn,' she said,
As she looked out the window and smiled,
'But relax and enjoy the whole session,
I won't be observed for a while!'

The heavens open

Picnic day, picnic day –
Just one hip, hip, and no hooray.
The skies have opened wide today,
The rain is pouring down!

Church picnic
Boggy field
Muddy shoes
Umbrella shields
Tree trunk huddle
Hoods tight
Lips blue
And faces white

Picnic day, picnic day –
Just one hip, hip, and no hooray.
The skies have opened wide today,
The rain is pouring down!

Curate smiles
Vicar frowns
Soggy sing-song
Voices drowned
Not a ray
Not a hope
Heavy sky
Children mope

Picnic day, picnic day –
Just one hip, hip, and no hooray.
The skies have opened wide today,
The rain is pouring down!

Rain in sheets
Blanket clouds
Bad dream
Thunder loud
Every year
No joking
St Mary's church
Gets a soaking

Picnic day, picnic day –
Just one hip, hip, and no hooray.
The skies have opened wide today,
The rain is pouring down!

An English holiday

It's raining again; the beach is wet,
Boats rock between the fishermen's nets.
We'd like to go home but Mum's mind is set –
We're staying here for the week.

The sky is angry and full of spite,
Tall waves explode like dynamite,
The lighthouse flashes both day and night –
But we're staying here for the week.

The fairground is shut, the pier's closed down,
The teashops are full in the centre of town,
The puddles are deeper than Dad's frozen frown –
But we're staying here for the week.

We've played every game back at the hotel,
We've joined dot-to-dot till we're dotty as well,
We haven't caught sight of crab, rock or shell –
But we're staying here for the week.

The deckchair attendant gives sigh after sigh,
The seagulls are hiding; you can't hear a cry,
And my brother and me are left wondering why –
We're staying here for the week!

Daydream

Stranded on an island, in the middle of the sea,
Is the teacher I dislike… the one who dislikes me.
She's pacing up and down and dodging coconuts,
And making up a bed inside a little wooden hut.
No ships are passing by, no planes are in the sky,
She'll have to stay for ages and watch the years go by.
She's far away from school, at least that's how it
    seems –
It's amazing what our minds can do when we sit and
    dream!

Glimpse

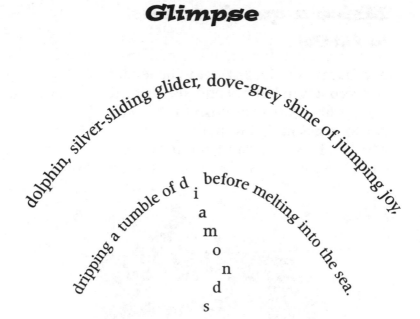

dolphin, silver-sliding glider, dove-grey shine of jumping joy,

dripping a tumble of d i a m o n d s before melting into the sea.

Make a quick guess
(a riddle)

My first is in swim but not in beneath,
My second's in hungry and also in teeth.
My third's in attack but isn't in blood,
My fourth is in rip but not in thud.
My fifth is in killer but isn't in cruel –
I can see you right now and I'm starting to drool.

(Answer: A shark.)

Warning

(a tongue twister)

Never be an enemy
To Emily anemone;
Her tentacles have tendency
To sling a sting of potency!

Piranha drama

The piranhas would be calmer,
And would never want to harm yer,
If the dishes for these fishes
Were as big as hungry wishes.

The mask

Buried in the scalloped sand,
Not so very far from land,
Is a crab that does not ask
For sunshine days in which to bask.
Instead, he hides from sunlight ray,
And bides his time till end of day.
Then, under cover of the night,
He wriggles out, a scary sight.
For, though he is but small and drab,
He looks a most mysterious crab.

Upon his back a mask* is etched,
With mouth and nose and eyes wide-stretched;
As you look down into the blue
It seems he's gazing back at you.
It's true that he could do no harm,
And shouldn't cause you much alarm.
It's true he looks a weedy crab,
His only crime to jab and grab.
Yet locals all avoid his glare –
An eerie, vacant, ghostly stare.

* The masked crab has face-like markings on its shell.

Diving for Daniel

Warm, salty water played against our cheeks,
Brushed over our shoulders and down our torsos.
Bubbles trailed like fairy dust.
This shallow dive had become a search.
Equipped with only snorkels and flippers,
We had become agents on a mission.
We were diving for Daniel.

Holidaymakers together, we worked as a team.
Like a school of fish, we wriggled in and out,
Flipped our tails, plunged and surfaced.

Daniel's small car had dropped from the dinghy;
His favourite car, his oldest car, his treasured car.
More snorkellers joined the cause, asked for details.
The shore was awash with sympathy.

Daniel sat humming comfort to himself,
Watching the water's surface for signs of a catch.
The sun would soon go down, and so water splashed
With limbs, urgently twisting and turning,
Diving for Daniel.

When hope was almost gone, and the water had
  calmed,
A single arm emerged from golden ripples –
The hand was tight-fisted and steady.
One by one, fingers were released
And the fist opened like an oyster shell.
There, inside, was a pearl of great worth.

Wreck

I am the wreck
That holds many secrets –
Of pirates and maidens,
And cannon explosions;
Of glittering treasure
And weapons aplenty.

I am the wreck
That could tell you some stories –
Of love, hate and envy,
Of greed, lust and power;
Of winning and losing,
And battles of will.

I am the wreck
That could unpack a history
Of age-old wrongdoing
That leads to destruction;
The rights and the wrongs,
The courage and fear.

I am the wreck
That is prodded and poked at,
Holds tightly to details
You dig and you scrape at;
But my secrets will stay
In the depths of my hull.

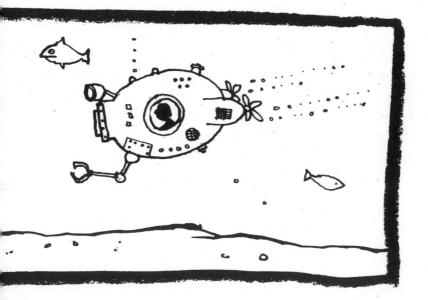

Freak

Nervously, she peeps from seagrasses,
Tail curled around a weed for anchorage.
She is peculiar, she knows.
Her horse head is out of place in a coral landscape.
Her long nose droops in shy submission.
Seaweed offers protection for her tissue-thin skin,
Caresses the curl of her tail, gently.
She would live more openly, more independently,
If her features were ordinary.
She would swim with confidence
If her shape had been designed with less
    imagination.
But instead she hides, unaware that,
At times, we all feel like seahorses,
With tissue-thin skin.

Zap

Quieter than thinking,
Quicker than blinking,
The chameleon's tongue goes ZAP!
And then a poor spider
Must wriggle inside her
While she searches again for a snack.

SUPER QUICK FREEZE-FRAME DRAWING

ZAP!

Armadillo pillow

Never use an armadillo
For your night-time pillow,
You'll never get a wink of sleep all night.
Armadillos are not springy
Like balloons and balls and dinghies,
And when you wake you'll get an awful fright!

Excuse

Just like a hungry panther,
This bad mood has stalked me.
It has hunted me down
Until I have given in.
Now I'm cornered. It glares at me,
Its evil, green eyes narrowing coldly.

I will skulk under its shadow until
I am consumed.
No amount of sunshine and singing
Can rescue me.

My teacher's as wild as a bison

My teacher's as wild as a bison,
She's charging around in a huff.
I think, from her pace
And the look on her face,
She's about to shout, 'I've had enough!'

Some say that she's overreacting,
Some say that she ought not to frown;
But 5B can be testing,
There's no time for resting,
5B could get anyone down!

There's Rachel, who could talk for England,
There's Simon, who won't say a word;
There's Uzma, who wriggles,
Persistently giggles
Till she knows for a fact she's been heard.

There's Peter, who thinks he's the teacher,
And interrupts Miss all the time;
And Clare, who sits frozen
If she isn't chosen,
Then sits in the corner and whines.

There's Abdul, who just never listens,
And constantly talks at the back.
There's Gemma, who'll cry
At the sight of a fly
Or a spider, or beetle, or gnat!

There's Laura, who never remembers
To bring what she needs for the day;
And Tom, who ignores
What rules are there for,
And gets into trouble each Play.

There's Jason, who likes to tell jokes
And bursts into laughter at will;
And then we have Kate,
Always fashionably late –
She invents her excuses with skill!

So my teacher's as wild as a bison,
And she has every reason to be;
Think I'll smile and be good,
As all nice children should,
So she doesn't come charging at me!

The Colorado diet
(a parody* of a playground rhyme)

One potato, two potato, three potato, four,
The Colorado beetle** has potatoes in her store.
Five potato, six potato, seven potato, eight,
She tucks in pretty quickly to the spuds upon her
plate.
Nine potato, ten potato, eleven potato, twelve,
She planned to start a diet; her plans have now been
shelved.
More potatoes, more potatoes, more potatoes, loads,
The Colorado beetle swallows hard and then
explodes!

* A parody is an imitation of another poem or story, done in a humorous way.
  Which playground rhyme is this a parody of?
** The Colorado beetle is very destructive to the potato plant.

Contaminated

(a haiku)

Acid rain falling –
God's tears of disappointment
Contaminated.

Polar problem

(a haiku)

The ice is melting –
A tide of carelessness brings
A flood of regret.

Pity

at a car boot sale

The elephant tusk* has sharp memories,
Its stories mix with car boot bric-a-brac.
Slender, narrowing, porcelain bow,
A flash of the wild on a wet English day.
Everyone looks, but nobody buys.
Some people stroke the bend of its back;
Some people feel the tip of its point.
But nobody buys this moon-slice of creature,
For the pity is too great.
The curling trunk is missing and the great,
    tent-flap ears.
The huge, grey cloud of wrinkles and cracks
Is only an echo blown on African winds.
So everyone looks, but nobody buys.
The pity is too great.
The pity is too great.

---

* Elephants are still hunted and killed for their ivory tusks. It is a very cruel and
  unnecessary trade.

Aslan rising

In the African dust and the shimmer of heat,
The lion hangs his patchy head,
His bloody nose resting on a large paw.
His mane, that once crashed like mighty waves
Around his royal face, is matted and flat,
Tufted into random sprigs of hair.
Stark ribs press their pattern through taut skin,
Rise and fall with the effort of his breathing.
He had fought long and hard;
Used all the tricks of combat;
Pretended to be a fearless foe;
But his age had got the better of him,
And his wounds are deep.
He accepts that the end is near,
That time is closing in, circling from above.
He can hear the low growl of death.
But I resist, deny the fading colour of his eyes,
And pray to see a miracle, like Aslan* rising.

* If you don't know who Aslan is, you need to read *The Lion, the Witch and the Wardrobe* by C. S. Lewis.

Potty

Hattie hippo dreamed all day
Of going to the city,
So she could dance upon a stage
In a tutu, pink and pretty.

One day she waved goodbye and then
She blew a parting kiss,
The other hippos all agreed,
'She's a hippo-potty-miss!'

That's entertainment

A crocodile
Can take a while
To work the dial
On his radio.

But once he's tuned in
You won't budge him
While he's listening
To the show.

Dancing bear*

(a sonnet)

Beneath his thinning brown and matted hair
Are eyes that stare with no desire to see.
He dances round and round the dusty square,
The blurring faces merge into a sea.
Stretched high on tired legs, his dance is skilled;
His training has equipped him to delight.
He acts the entertainer, as he's billed,
He sways his head, as taught, from left to right.
The leather muzzle, on his tender head,
Hides well the scars that mark his haggard face.
A ring has made his nostrils raw and red,
And yet he dresses misery with grace.
    I feel the hopeless anguish of his trance –
    There is no beauty in this painful dance.

* Bears are still captured in some countries, and taught to 'dance' to earn
money for their captors. They are trained and treated in a cruel way.

Gus

(a limerick)

There was a young walrus called Gus
Who decided to go out and busk,
He danced (with a hobble)
Till his blubber did wobble,
And plucked a guitar with his tusks.

Wild about teeth

God is just wild about teeth,
He's given them out liberally.
Through the whole of creation,
In every nation,
He's distributed choppers for free!

The animal kingdom is shining
With teeth that glint in the sun.
The whiteness is blinding
When molars are grinding,
And incisors flash through the gums.

Jaguars, lions and panthers,
All have a zigzaggy smile;
And sharks in the ocean
Could do a promotion
For saw blades that sever with style!

A crocodile's teeth are so spiky;
The ends are as sharp as a barb.
When he opens his jaws,
Run fast, never pause,
Don't allow him to catch you off guard.

The jungle, the desert, the forest –
Each place has its fair share of teeth:
Be they molars in canines,
Or incisors in bovines*
And bunnies that hop on the heath.

So next time you look in the mirror,
Open your jaws and reflect –
On the wondrous enamel
You share with a camel,
And the teeth it's designed to protect.

* Bovine is another word for a cow.

More poetry from Lion Children's Books

All Things Weird and Wonderful   *Stewart Henderson*

Breaking the Rules   *Coral Rumble*

Crazy Classrooms and Secret Staffrooms   *Paul Cookson*

Dad, You're Not Funny   *Steve Turner*

The Day I Fell Down the Toilet   *Steve Turner*

Imagining Things   *Kenneth Steven*

I Was Only Asking   *Steve Turner*

The Moon Has Got His Pants On   *Steve Turner*

Poems and Prayers for a Better World   *Su Box and Felicity Henderson*

Staying Out Late, Playing Out Late   *Paul Cookson*

What Will You Wear to Go Swimming?   *Lois Rock*

Whispering in God's Ear   *Alan MacDonald*

Who Left Grandad at the Chip Shop?   *Stewart Henderson*

www.lionhudson.com